MAIL ORDER BRIDE

A Bride for Aaron

SUN RIVER BRIDES
BOOK 8

KARLA GRACEY

Dedication

I dedicate this book to my mother, as she was the one who kept urging me to write, and without her enthusiasm I would never written and published my books.

Contents

Chapter One

Deep, booming laughter and rapturous applause filled the air as young Christopher completed a new trick his step-mother, Emily, had taught him to do with Claude and bowed deeply. Aaron, having only arrived at the farm a few moments before had found himself marveling at how calmly Matthew had watched as the boy tumbled off the donkey's back, had been apt to go and pick the boy up and dust him down. But he had soon realized it was just a part of an act when his brother put a hand out to stop him, and Claude had wandered over, nudged the lad and then taking his shirt in his teeth picked him up and carried him towards them where he dropped Chris unceremoniously into his Papa's lap. "I cannot believe how clever that mule is," Aaron said to Emily.

"He was always far better at being a circus performer than I was," she admitted. "Chris is so talented, has learned tricks in moments that it took me a lifetime to master."

"He certainly seems to enjoy it," Matthew said. "I can't tell you how scared I was the first time I saw Christopher roll off his back and onto the floor!"

"All I had to do was to teach Christopher how to land," Emily admitted. "After that he and Claude have been developing their tricks alone. I know my family will be very impressed when next they visit, will try and whisk them off to Boston to be in the circus, but I think we should keep them both here a while longer," she said, ruffling Chris's curls as Matthew hugged his boy close.

Claude nudged at Matthew, and Aaron laughed as the donkey seemed to grin at them as though he was proud of his antics. "You know where it is," Matthew said to him. Claude went straight for his coat pocket, and extracted a carrot. Content, he wandered back towards his paddock and crunched his reward. He clearly believed his work was done for the day.

"I can imagine they would. They truly do make a good partnership and I am sure people would be glad to pay out their hard earned pennies to see them perform. But, Chris does seem a little young yet." Aaron agreed.

"Emily was performing years younger," Matthew said proudly. She blushed.

"But I grew up in the circus, and my family were all around me. It can be a hard life, and he should be old enough to choose it for himself – though I know he would be much loved and taken care of by his Uncle and his Grandmama. But, we are too selfish, want him to be here with us – he has an important role to fulfill soon after all." She looked down at the boy who grinned at her.

"I am going to be a big brother," he announced proudly, his little chest all puffed out.

"Well, that is news indeed," Aaron said. "I am sure you will be a very good big brother, you have a wonderful example to follow. Your Papa is the best big brother in the world."

"But Claude will always be mine. Mama says the baby will be too little to play with him for a long time, but I don't think Claude would mind. He is very gentle." Aaron smiled at how grown up the little boy was trying to sound.

"Claude really is a character isn't he, and as much a part of the family as any of us?" Aaron marveled. Emily smiled. She was obviously proud of the animal, and he truly could understand why.

"Come Chris, you should wash and change before supper," she encouraged the boy. Matthew reached up and kissed his father before he got down. "We shall leave you two to catch up a little. You must have much to talk about."

"Uncle Aaron?"

"Yes Chris?"

"Will you be staying long?"

"I don't know. That depends upon a lot of things, but I certainly hope to," he said looking into the boy's serious little face.

"I hope so too. I like having you here, and so does Daddy. We have been very excited ever since we heard you were on your way."

"Well that is good to know."

He hadn't ever thought of himself as the paternal type before, but seeing his brother so settled and happy was having an effect on Aaron. As a journalist he had travelled the length and breadth of the country, and had always believed that he enjoyed his life that way. But, even in the short time he had been here with Matthew and Emily, in Sun River, he was beginning to see that there were positives to being settled too. He adored his young nephew; he was so full of life and curiosity and wanted to know everything anyone was prepared to teach him. He had begun to consider what being a father might be like, whether a child of his own was something he wanted. He was almost certain now that it was. He truly had expected that being in the same house as the boy for more than a few hours would have had him tearing his hair out in frustration, but the opposite was true. He couldn't wait to spend more time with the lad.

"Well, would you stay?" Matthew asked once Emily and Chris were inside. "I know you only intended to be here for a few days before heading off to find a story somewhere, but I'd love to have my little brother nearby."

"I hadn't thought about it Matty, I've been on the road so long it is what seems normal to me. But, you have a wonderful life here. I have to admit you are making me a little jealous. I never thought I would yearn for hearth and home, but if it contained a talented donkey and a woman as good as Emily I think I could be convinced," he joked. Matthew looked at him, staring deep into his eyes. His brother had always been able to read him like a book, and Aaron was used to the scrutiny, but today it made him feel a little self-conscious.

"Aaron, I miss you," he said finally. "And I think Sun River needs someone like you. We don't have our own newspaper, and it would be good to have something more up to date with our local news than the newspapers from Great Falls and Billings."

"You truly think there is a need? Sun River is pretty sleepy. I can't imagine much happens here," he said with a rueful grin.

"Are you sure? Just because things appear to be quiet it

doesn't mean it is – you of all people should know that!"

"I do. Often the quietest places hide the best stories, but other than an influx of Boston wives, there really isn't much happening here."

"Other than the rumors that Sheriff Partlin is crooked? Or the unexplained disappearance of three actors from the theatre this week? Or the possibility that we may have the next Governor of the State living in our midst? None of that enough for you?" Matthew chuckled.

"Well, when you put it like that, then yes, I suppose there possibly is scope for a weekly newspaper I suppose. But, a man cannot make a living from such a small print run as would be required here."

"I can always use help here. In fact the farm will be up for sale as soon as I have paid off the debts I took on to build the theatre – though the sooner I could sell it the sooner I could pay those off too!" Matthew said. Aaron snorted.

"You do not want me here. I would have your farm in tatters in no time. I am not cut out for a life on the land and you know it!"

"Neither was I when I came out here, but I learnt. There are good people all around and they help each other out. I'd be nearby to give you advice." They both sat quietly, thinking for a moment. Aaron was grateful for his brother's support, but it was not right for either of them for him to accept it without taking his share of the responsibility and he was more than sure that owning a farm was not something that was right for him.

"There is always MacAlpine's campaign for Governor?" Matthew said suddenly. His face lit up. "The more I think of it, the better it is as an opportunity for you. You have contacts all over the State, you know all the people who would need to know him, and see him. You understand how politics works."

"I do, and it is why I have spent much of my life reporting it, rather than getting involved in it. I could never support any of the politicians I have met. They seem wonderful to your face, but dig only a little way beneath the surface there is always something unpleasant."

"Gideon is a good man. I wouldn't suggest you support anyone I don't believe in – but that is his problem."

"What do you mean?"

"He is too good. He genuinely wishes to seek election to make changes that benefit us all. He hopes to win because he is the best candidate."

"You and I both know that the best candidate rarely wins. You cannot win if you have scruples," Aaron said sadly.

"Indeed, but we need men like him making the decisions that matter. Good men can make a change."

"There aren't enough of them, that is true, but that is because even good men become bad men once they are in positions of power and influence."

"I know you are cynical, and I don't blame you given what you have seen. But will you at least meet him?"

"Of course, but meeting someone and agreeing to help them are two very different things." His brother nodded. But though he had misgivings about all of his brother's suggestions, he was glad that there were at least options should he decide to stay. He hadn't come here thinking of it, but the more they sat out there, on the broad porch, watching the sun set over the mountains he felt at peace for the first time in too many years. He could live here, in Sun River. It already felt like home, and the only people in the world that he cared about were here. But, there would be much to think on if he were to do so.

Emily emerged from the screen door, Chris trailing behind her. "Supper is ready," she said. "I'm sorry, I did not mean to eavesdrop, but I overheard your conversation from in the kitchen. Have you considered the school? Myra is looking for a schoolmaster."

"I think I would prefer teaching to entering politics," Aaron said with a smile. "But I have no experience, and am not sure I could cope with more than one child at a time."

"You will never know unless you try," she said with a grin. "Chris seems to have taken to you, and he is not always so outgoing. If you can win over our stubborn little man then the other local children would be easy. But come on in and eat, you can think about it for as long as you like. We will be seeing Myra and Carlton tomorrow at the Harvest Supper, you can talk to her then."

"If I did not know better, I would say that the three of you are conspiring to tether me down," he said, picking up Chris and raising him high above his head. The little boy squealed his pleasure.

"We love you Uncle Aaron," he said in his sweet and clear voice. Aaron squeezed him tightly against his chest.

"That is very good to know lad."

After supper he made his way out onto the porch alone. He sank into one of the rockers and thought about the conversation they had shared earlier. He was surprised to even be considering staying here. Sun River was so small. He was used to big cities. He loved winkling out corruption and laying it bare for all to see. He simply couldn't see that there would be that much here in Sun River for him to investigate. But, he also had to admit that he had begun to find the monotony of people's depravity was becoming dull. He found himself reporting on the same things, done by different people, in different places. Scandal seemed to be anything but shocking to him after all his years working in the newspaper trade. He was never surprised, never stunned by the things people could do to one another.

He could hear Emily and Matthew laughing together inside. He could see just how much pleasure their relationship was giving them. Their work together at the theatre gave them both much pleasure, and their skills and knowledge seemed to complement one another perfectly. The little touches, and soft looks they shared when they believed nobody was looking spoke volumes about the passion they shared and he was envious. Even here at the farm, they worked in tandem to ensure work got done and the land stayed in good heart, though he knew they hoped to move into Sun River itself as soon as they could.

He stood and stretched. His body felt tired. Too much travelling and uncomfortable beds in hotels had left his body feeling less than its best. He could already feel the difference in his health that the fresh mountain air was making to his wellbeing. Good food and a comfortable home would build him back up. But even now he wasn't sure he wished to return to his old life. He needed a new challenge, and he needed to feel as he had since he had been here: welcomed and loved. His life had become so lonely. When he heard about the friends that his brother had made here in Sun River, the bonds that he had built so successfully, Aaron began to doubt the choices he had made in his own life.

He wandered over to the paddock. Claude plodded over to the gate and allowed him to scratch his nose. "Claude, you were a big city boy, how did you make the change? It must have been quite a shock, a big star like you." Claude brayed softly. It sounded as if he was laughing. Aaron looked at him. The animal often seemed so clever, as if he truly understood everything his family said. "You think I'm being a fool to ask such a question? What do you suggest? Should I stay?" Claude nodded vigorously. "You're biased. They've set you up to work on me," he joked. But though it seemed such a simple decision to make, there were things in his past that could make it hard for him if he chose to remain in one place, and the last thing he wanted to do was to put his family in danger. The donkey nuzzled at his chest, encouraging Aaron to stroke his cheeks and his neck. It felt so wonderful to be accepted, to be wanted though, and he knew he had even more than that here. He had love. "It's working Claude. You've done well."

"He really makes a lot of sense," Emily said, walking softly towards them. "I've always told him my troubles."

"He is definitely a good listener," Aaron said with a grin. "Gives good advice too."

"Always," Emily chuckled as she hugged her old friend around his hairy grey neck. "We would all love you to stay Aaron, but it has to be your choice."

"I am considering it. I do find it harder and harder to stay in my profession. I would very much like to believe in the goodness of people again. I sadly see precious little of that in my work."

"Aaron, forgive me if this is a little presumptuous, especially given how short a period of time I have known you – but I think you may be looking for your place, and most especially for love." He began to protest, but she shushed him quickly. "I saw you watching us, you had a look I recognized all too well – it was the look I often had as I watched my family and friends in the Circus. I wanted what they had so desperately, love of what they did and of each other. I never felt I fitted in because I didn't share their passions. But I found it here, that love and the feeling of being a part of something. Maybe you might too. So here." She thrust a newspaper at him. "It's how Matthew and I met. Maybe there is somebody in there for you too." He looked at the page she had left it open at. The Matrimonials advertisements. He laughed out loud.

"You think I should advertise for a wife?" he asked incredulously.

"No, I think you should respond to this advertisement, here," she said pointing at one she had circled.

> *Young Woman of Boston, seeks educated man to correspond, with a view to matrimony. The subscriber is strong, a capable cook and fine housekeeper and is good with children. Respondents should be kind and gentle, with a good heart. A sense of adventure would be most highly valued. All responses should apply to Box 643, The Boston Globe*

"She sounds most practical," he said wryly.

"I think she sounds ideal for you. She can make you a home, and teach you how to live in it - but I think you will also need a wife who will understand that you are always going to be haring off to investigate something - whatever else you may decide to do in your future. If she already appreciates a sense of adventure, I think it may be a very good start." She winked at him and sashayed back inside.

Aaron shook his head in disbelief. The woman was incorrigible. No wonder his brother adored her so much. He re-read the advertisement, and found himself wondering what kind of a woman would write such a thing, would set herself up to potentially move across the country just so she could be wed. He had so often scorned the people who advertised in such a way, had believed it impossible to build a genuine relationship from such inauspicious beginnings – but his brother and sister-in-law and so many of their friends gave him the proof that he was wrong. Maybe he should respond, it would at least help him to answer his questions? Maybe he could write an article about it and submit it to the Globe? At best he might find the love of his life and at worst he would be able to make a few dollars from the experience. He gave Claude one last pat and headed back inside to write a response. He was intrigued as to what he would receive in return.

Chapter Two

Frederica kneaded a large mound of dough at her Aunt's kitchen table. Usually she found making bread to be an experience that helped her to clear her mind, but today as she pounded the dough and shaped it into loaves she couldn't help wondering if she would ever receive a response to her advertisement. She loved Uncle Frederick, for whom she had been named, but Aunt Marian was a hard task master. She seemed unable to understand that Frederica could still be devastated by the loss of her Mother and Father. She was always so terse and curt whenever she found Frederica looking anything less than content.

It had only been twenty-three long months since they had been lost at sea; their bodies never found after the sinking of the boat they had been enjoying a pleasure cruise in around Boston harbor. Aunt Marian did not seem to think there had been anything unfinished about burying empty caskets, the thought that without their bodies it was so much harder to accept. But Frederica still struggled to understand why her loving and kind parents had been taken from her in such a way, to be at peace with her loss. Every day it got a little easier to bear, but it never stopped hurting.

Her Aunt and Uncle were her only relatives, and had been kind enough to offer her a place on their upstate farm following the

KARLA GRACEY

tragedy. She had nowhere else to go, and her family had left her with little; they had not been wealthy people. She had adapted as best she could to the new rhythm of life on the farm, and had become adept at milking the herd of dairy cows, making butter and cheese. It helped her to keep herself busy, to stop her mind from pondering her losses. She had surprised herself to find that she actually enjoyed it and did not miss the hustle and bustle of the city at all.

"Well my darling girl, "Uncle Frederick said jovially as he entered the kitchen. His vast girth took up much of the doorway, and his ruddy cheeks were always stretched into a happy smile. "Who is writing to you from the newspaper?" She almost dropped the tray of bread she had been about to pop into the oven.

"There is a letter for me?" she asked nervously. It was strange, she had been waiting for this moment, yet now that it was here she could hardly bear it. Butterflies began to beat their wings mercilessly in her belly, and she could feel her breath getting shorter and more shallow.

"No my darling, there is stack of them a foot high!" he chuckled.

"No!" she gasped. "Do not tease me so."

"I would not. But, I cannot help but be intrigued. You have lived here for almost two years now, and barely received a thing from anyone. "

"Will you promise not to tell Aunt Marian? I could not bear the snide comments she would be bound to make," she admitted. She knew that Uncle Frederick would do so, he always appeared to be a happy man but he did not have the happiest marriage. He and Aunt Marian had married because their families' farms had been adjoining and Grandfather had been determined to gain the lush grazing land their neighbors held. They had not been blessed with children, and this had made the already unhappy Aunt Marian become bitter. Frederica was determined that she would not be sold off in marriage in the same way, though she knew Uncle Frederick would never force her to anything. But, she had determined that she would make her own life, and this was the first step towards that.

"When does she ever speak to me, other than to call me for supper?" he asked and she could hear the sadness in his voice. Frederica was sure that he loved his wife, and struggled to cope with her ambivalence, but he was too kind to ever push himself upon her.

10

The sadness in the house was tangible. She vowed to make sure that whoever she chose, her husband would have to possess the courage to speak up and tell her his troubles. She did not want to be alone in her own home.

"I placed an advertisement, in the Matrimonials section," she confessed. She found herself unable to look him in the eye, and fussed around checking the bread was correctly placed in the oven before she turned back to him.

"I should be surprised, but I am not. You are a woman of uncharacteristic courage my darling, I should have known you would take your destiny into your own hands. I am sorry our home is not more welcoming to you."

"It is not that," she said, trying to placate him. "I do long for a family of my own and I have nobody to speak for me but myself."

"I will always speak for you, would give you everything that is in my power to do so – and though I know that you believe your Aunt would not, she would. She loves you in her own way. You just remind her that she was unable to have children of her own and that is hard for her."

"I can understand that, and I do try to remember it always. Now, where are my letters," she said feeling oddly sad, and very excited all at once.

She dusted the flour from her hands, and followed him into his study. The pile was indeed much larger than she had ever expected. She prayed that somewhere in there that there would be a man she wanted to know more of, a man she could consider. Her Uncle's assurance that Aunt Marian did care for her did not change how hard it was to live under her roof. She wasn't prepared to take the blame any longer for the hardships Aunt Marian had been forced to bear. None of them was her fault, and it was unfair of her to take her unhappiness out on Frederica.

She sank into her Uncle's elegant leather chair and began to leaf through them. "I shall leave you alone," Uncle Frederick said kindly, patting her affectionately on the shoulder. "Choose well, and if you wish my advice I will always be here for you." He kissed her on the forehead and shut the door behind him. Frederica was astounded, as she counted under her breath. Twenty-eight men had written to her. She leaned back in the chair, and raised her hands to her face. Now she was faced with the reality of the situation it seemed completely unreal. She simply did not know where to start. However would she be able to choose between these men? What criteria mattered most to her in a future husband? What was she looking for? She suddenly doubted her reasons for ever placing the advertisement, her judgment and her sanity.

She opened the first letter in the pile, and began to read. She felt it only right to read every word that these men had labored over, it was only fair she give them an equal chance to impress her. But it was soon clear that many of the respondents could barely write a sentence, let alone make it interesting enough to make her wish to write back to them. She began to despair as she worked her way through the first ten letters. Not one of them asked her about herself, or cared enough to have even read her advertisement carefully. They seemed to have simply responded, thinking she must be desperate, and would therefore consider anybody.

She threw the growing pile of rejected suitors into the fire, and leant wearily against the mantel as they curled up and burst into flames. Why had she ever thought that she could change her life this way? It was hopeless. She moved back to the desk and picked up the remaining, unopened, envelopes and began to feed them into the fire. There was no point in reading them, they would all be the same, she was sure of it. "Frederica," her Aunt called. She wiped a tear from her eye and put the remaining letters back on the desk. She opened the door.

"Yes Aunt Marian?" she said to the haughty looking woman standing in the hallway.

"Your Uncle said you were in here. How much longer does the bread need to be in the oven?" she asked. Frederica looked over her shoulder at the large hallway clock.

"Oh my, thank you for reminding me," she gasped and hurried to the kitchen. "It would have been burnt had you not called." She pulled the loaves out and turned to place them on the cooling racks on the table, expecting to see her Aunt had followed her to give her a lecture about wasting expensive ingredients. But Aunt Marian had not done so. "Aunt?" she asked as she headed back towards the office. She blushed, and felt ashamed as she saw the older woman fingering the pile of letters.

"You have many friends at the newspaper?" she asked, her face icy.

"No, none."

"Then why so many letters?" Frederica sighed, she would have to tell the truth and so she did. Aunt Marian's face remained impassive, aloof. "I see," she said finally. "Have you found a suitable match? I presume there must have been something that intrigued you sufficiently to make you forget your chores."

"They were all terrible. In fact I was about to burn the remaining ones as I have given up hope that there will be anybody worth responding to, if the first eleven were anything to judge by."

"I think that rash. What if the man you are destined to be with is amongst these?" Aunt Marian asked. If Frederica hadn't known her so well, she would have sworn that a smile was playing around her thin lips, but that couldn't be. Aunt Marian never smiled.

"I doubt it."

"Nonetheless, you should continue to read them. I shall go and make a start on the milking for you." Frederica was now stunned. Her aunt never offered to help her out with her chores, and she certainly hadn't set foot in the milking sheds since Frederica had come to live on the farm.

"Why?" she said. "I am sorry, that sounded terrible. But, you have always seemed to dislike me, seen me as a burden you were forced to bear, yet you are being so kind now?"

"Dear Frederica. I am not heartless, though I know I may seem that way. I was once a young girl with dreams of a happy marriage myself. I suppose I could have tried harder to make the one that was forced upon me work better, but I wished to punish everyone for making me wed a man I did not choose. I think it quite possible that the only people who have been hurt by my actions are myself and your Uncle. He is a good man, and I have made his life a misery – when I wished to hurt my own Papa and his."

"Aunt Marian, it isn't too late. Uncle Frederick loves you – I am sure of it. He would welcome you with open arms if you were ever to show him the slightest indications of affection."

"I cannot. It is not proper for a woman to behave so," Aunt Marian said primly.

"Nonsense," Frederica said. "You are married, hardly a young virgin awaiting her first beau. If you want your life to be better then you have to make it so." The words were barely out of her mouth before she wished she could unsay them, but her Aunt did not react in the way she would have expected to her bluntness.

"As you have?" Aunt Marian asked, raising a single eyebrow quizzically.

"As I tried, yes."

"Then, will you take your own advice and continue to see that attempt through?"

"I shall, if you will try and make your marriage a better one for both you and Uncle Frederick. If I find a husband, it would be reassuring to know that I have not left you both here, unhappy and alone when you both wish for something else, something more, something better."

"You are a good girl. I am sorry I have been unkind. I was just so jealous of your mother. Everything seemed to come so easily for her."

"I can assure you it did not. She and Papa worked hard to make their marriage work. If it looked differently on the outside, then that showed how good they both were at hiding the cracks."

"I suppose we never know what is truly happening between closed doors do we?" Aunt Marian mused. "I shall go and milk the cows." She turned and hurried from the room. Frederica was sure that she had seen a tear in her eye, and that though she had admitted to much in their short conversation, that was just a step too far for Aunt Marian. She found herself hoping that what she had revealed was true, that her Aunt and Uncle would find that it was never too late to reconcile and even build a wonderful and loving marriage. She sat back down and with a sigh opened the first letter.

It took her a further seven to find a man who sounded even vaguely interesting, and another five to find a man she wanted to respond to. His elegant script sprawled lightly across the page. He sounded perfect.

Dear Young Lady of Boston,

I am writing in response to your intriguing advertisement in The Globe. I can only hope that your situation is not a desperate one. I would hate to think that you find yourself in a predicament that forces you to take such drastic measures as to advertise for a husband. I prefer to hope that you are rather searching for love in some new and unconventional way. I admire women who take responsibility for their own lives, their own happiness and I am blessed to know of many people who have been successful in finding wonderful relationships this way.

I am a journalist. I will confess, when I first considered responding to you I did it with a view to maybe writing an article about my experience, but each time I read your words and then try and form my own I feel less inclined to do so. I am a lonely man. I have spent much of my life travelling up and down the country in search of a good story. It is time to stop searching and recording other people's lives, and to start experiencing my own.

I have a brother, and I am currently staying with him here in Montana. Sun River is a lovely spot, with mountains all around and I find myself eager to stay – though if you would prefer I can move back East to be near your family and friends if you would prefer. (Of course, this is presumptuous of me, that you would pick me and marry me! I apologize most profusely for my arrogance.)

He is in the process of selling his farm, and though I confess to knowing little about it, I find myself considering purchasing it from him. He did not know anything when he came here, so how hard could it be to learn? It is in a goodly spot, and has good yields. He has kept in good heart, whatever that means!

I do pray that you will consider corresponding with me, I am eager to get to know you better and hope you will think we might suit.

Yours most humbly
Aaron Simmons

Frederica sighed contentedly. He sounded perfect, with the intelligence she craved and the desire to make a new start to a life no longer fulfilling him – as she was searching to do herself. She reached automatically for a sheet of paper from her Uncle's drawer, and began to compose a reply. With every word she wrote, she prayed that she had chosen wisely.

Chapter Three

Aaron had discovered that he was a fast learner. As he pitched hay into the barn, he couldn't help humming happily to himself. His body had never ached so much in his entire life, but he felt clean and content in the honest toil he undertook each day. "We'll make a farmer of you after all," Matthew teased him as he entered the barn and took up a pitch fork himself.

"You just might," he admitted, leaning against his fork, taking a breath for a moment. "Matthew, I'd like to discuss buying the farm from you after all. I've led a frugal life, most of my earnings I have saved over the years. I think I could afford to purchase the place from you."

"You should look into gaining the land adjacent too," Matthew said. "The Homestead Act means you can claim land – up to 160 acres. There are two ways in which you can gain legal title to it, proving up or outright purchase after six months. It is how I got this place."

"I shall have to look into that indeed," Aaron said. "What does proving up the land entail?"

"You have to work and live on the land for five years. It can be tough. The first five years are the hardest, as you are taking land never before put to the plough, or to grazing and making it good. But, you still have to do the work if you take the purchase option too, so I think it is wisest to prove up."

"How much would it cost to buy, do you know?"

"When I moved here the cost was $1.25 an acre and a $10 filing fee."

"That sounds more than reasonable, but would I be able to claim if I have already purchased land in Montana?"

"I do not know, but there is a lawyer in Great Falls who specializes in Homesteading. I can take you there so you can talk to him. We can wait for you to buy the farm if you want it too."

"I could not ask that of you, what if I have to wait the full five years?"

"You can still work the farm, just not own it! We can share the profits. But are you truly sure you want to become a farmer?"

"No, but I am beginning to come around to the idea. I like working outdoors, but I noticed that there is no dairy herd nearby? Maybe I could fill that gap. I am just exploring the options right now. The work at the school would be only a few hours a week at most, and the costs to set up a newspaper are prohibitive, and with such a small area of distribution it simply wouldn't be cost effective yet – though if Sun River continues to grow it might be in time. I do not wish to enter politics. I have met enough crooks in my life and have no desire to mingle with them by choice – even though your man is one of the rare few that is not yet corrupt."

"So, staying is a definite possibility?" Matthew asked hopefully.

"I think so," Aaron admitted. "I like it here, and I am tired of having no place to call home." His brother clapped him on the back and then pulled him into a bear hug.

"I am so glad," he said beaming. "We did not want to have to say goodbye."

The sound of a cart pulling up outside made them both turn. Emily was busy at the theatre, a new production was in rehearsal and so she was in town most days to ensure that the director had everything he needed. She often returned home exasperated, and it would appear that today was not any different. She stormed into the barn, her face as black as thunder. "How is dear Mr Lafarge today?" Matthew asked, trying to suppress a grin.

"The man is impossible. I shall be glad when he is gone.

Thankfully the play only has a short run, otherwise I should be in fear for my sanity," she said, clearly infuriated.

"What does he demand today?" Aaron asked. So far he had asked for fresh flowers in his office every day, an entire roast fowl to be prepared for his lunch each day – and never the same kind to be served two days in a row, and numerous other little things that were simply ridiculous.

"He wishes me to hire some rigging from one of the theatres in New York, apparently ours is not suitable and he does not trust Ardloe to be able to create something suitable in time."

"Did you not explain that it would take longer to have something shipped from New York?"

"Of course I did, and that Ardloe is a genius, but the man will not be told. I am going to have to fire him. The theatre will go bankrupt simply because of his demands on this one production."

"But, who will we be able to hire at such short notice?" Matthew said anxiously. "We only have a week until curtain up."

"I will have to do it, otherwise there will be no profit at all," Emily said.

"But you do not have the time," her husband said, "and have you ever directed anything before?"

"No, but I do know the play well and the actors know what they are doing. It cannot be so hard. Maybe if I had some help?" she said flirtatiously, reaching up and kissing him.

"I could pop down from time to time, but…"

"We both can. Matthew we have both attended the theatre often, we can see what works and what doesn't," Aaron said. Emily smiled at him.

"Thank you, I would be ever so glad of your support and suggestions." She turned to go inside. "Oh, I almost forgot. A letter from Boston, for you Aaron," she said turning back and giving him a wink.

"Thank you Emily," he said, amused at the pride in her voice that he had taken her advice.

"I hope she is lovely," she teased. Matthew watched the interplay between his brother and his wife with interest, but could not stop the look of confusion it brought about. They laughed at him, but neither bothered to enlighten him. Aaron could not testify as to Emily's reasons, but for now he personally wished to be able to get to know the mysterious advertiser without his brother getting too excited on his behalf. "Will you both excuse me for a while?" he said, and disappeared out of the barn before either could gainsay him.

He had long since discovered a quiet copse of trees at the end of the main paddock. He often made his way there when he longed for a little peace and solitude. He sank down onto the soft grass and lay on his back for a moment gazing up at the sky. It was not long before Claude came to investigate, and he was happy to spend a few moments fondling the curious animal's nose, and scratching lightly behind his long ears. "Well, she wrote back my friend," he said to the animal showing him the letter. Claude harrumphed softly and began cropping away at the grass. "You are right, why should it matter to you?" Aaron laughed.

He had expected to feel excited, maybe even a little anxious if he were to receive a reply, but he felt peculiarly calm – as if this was just another part of the puzzle of his life that was about to slot into place. He couldn't explain why he had such a good feeling about it, or why he was sure that this young woman and he would suit, but he did. He opened the envelope slowly and eased out the letter.

Dear Mr Simmons,

I cannot tell you how grateful I was to receive your letter. You would not believe the caliber of many of the responses I received. I was astounded that so many people would reply without having even read my advertisement carefully. I can certainly testify that very few had any education, let alone a good one!

I was intrigued when you said you are a journalist. I took a day and went to Boston where I went to the library to try and find as many of your pieces as I could. You have led a most exciting life if you have truly been chasing such stories across the country. To be so acquainted with a world of vice and danger must have been both thrilling and more than a little frightening I would imagine. I would imagine you have probably made some enemies along the way too, though I do hope that is not the case. Your writing is both eloquent and highly detailed. I found it most enjoyable, though often macabre!

I am glad that you think you may have found a place where you wish to rest, somewhere you may learn to call home. To have family is a blessing too precious to waste. Sadly I lost my parents in a tragic accident, but my Uncle Frederick was kind enough to take me in. For much of my time here I have not seen eye to eye with my Aunt Marian, but in recent weeks she seems to have thawed – not just to me but towards my Uncle too. I am glad of this, I think they may finally be learning to love one another, though they have been married for over twenty-eight years.

I have no siblings. I envy you a loving brother. I always wished to be part of a large family, but it was not to be. I hope that one day I will be able to have many children of my own. I never want a child of mine to feel the loneliness I did as a child. But, I am not unhappy I do hope you will believe this, though my words may make you think otherwise.

My Uncle is a dairy farmer, and I have grown to love living in the countryside. I have won awards for my cheese and butter making, and I find I truly enjoy the simplicity of milking and churning. My mind can so often go off on tangents, and I am prone to worries. I find that such tasks help to calm me, to soothe those thoughts away. I thought that I would miss the city when I moved here, but I was happy to find I did not. I got the feeling from your words that you are finding much the same thing.

Whilst in the library, I looked at pictures of Montana. It does indeed look most beautiful, the mountains so majestic. I can entirely understand why it had begun to work its magic upon you. I do hope that it continues to do so, that you choose to settle in Sun River with your family. I got the strangest feeling that being with them is making you much more content than your career has. I am most sorry for my impertinence!

I should very much like to meet with you, would like you to consider me as a possible bride for you as you begin your new life. My Uncle would happily escort me to Montana. I think he wishes to retire, and is looking to find somewhere beautiful to do so. I would not be surprised if he sold up the farm here and followed me if I were to move to Sun River!

I do not wish to scare you with the idea of me and my family turning up on your doorstep, will await your invitation should you wish to meet with me.

Yours most hopefully
Frederica Milton

Aaron smiled as he imagined this young woman sitting at a table, writing this effervescent missive. It amused him that she had investigated him, had found some of his articles and was more than flattered that she had liked them. But, he was stunned at her perception, that she had spotted the potential his work had for creating enemies. He certainly had made his fair share over the years. But, he was sure that none of them would pursue him further if he were to leave his journalism behind. None would follow him to Sun River, they would not even think of such a sleepy backwater as being his home he was sure.

He liked that she was inquisitive, that she so clearly adapted well to new things and that she already had skills in dairy farming. The more he thought upon his future, the more he was sure that it would be the most lucrative option available to him if he were to remain here. There were many farms, many ranchers, even a number of large sheep herds in the area – but there was no dairy herd. He had spent some time with Mack, herding his cattle, and he had found an unexpected tenderness towards the gentle creatures with their liquid brown eyes. But ranching did not appeal to him. He did not want to spend days, even weeks out on the trail taking his animals to and from markets, did not want to have to worry about where to find them. He liked the idea of neatly fenced fields full of happy cows, near to home.

Frederica could bring him the knowhow he needed, and if her Uncle did indeed follow her to Montana, he would have a fount of knowledge on his doorstep. It should not be a reason to marry a woman, but he couldn't help thinking that Fate had taken some steps in his direction for once. He wanted to meet her, wanted to know if they would suit – because so far everything was telling him that she might just be his perfect woman: practical, though clearly passionate; skilled and able to learn quickly; enthusiastic and fun. What more could any man ask for?

Chapter Four

Frederica nervously awaited a response. As soon as she had mailed her reply she had been hit by a torrent of anxieties. She hoped that she had not scared him away with her talk of wanting a large family, or that her Uncle was considering moving to stay near her. She had been surprised herself when he had taken her aside in the dairy one day and told her so. They had both wept as he spoke of his sadness at losing his last link to his beloved brother. But she did not know if he had even mentioned his proposal to Aunt Marian and that worried her. The pair had been showing signs of an improved relationship in recent weeks, and she did not want him to jeopardize his own chances for a happy marriage because he wished to be near to her.

She almost pounced upon her Uncle when she saw him entering the kitchen, brandishing a letter at her. "Thank you," she said, suddenly feeling giddy.

"I shall hope the man has sense," Uncle Frederick said softly patting her on the arm, then sitting himself down for breakfast. Aunt Marian served him his eggs, and even smiled at him. Frederica couldn't help herself, she kissed them both on the cheek.

"I am so happy that you are getting on so much better," she said as she ran out of the room to the privacy of her Aunt's parlor.

She sank into the comfortable armchair her Aunt sat in when doing the darning, and felt the warmth of the fire through her plain muslin gown.

> *Dear Miss Milton,*
>
> *I am so glad that you chose to correspond with me. By the sound of it you were inundated with options!*
>
> *I will not beat around the bush, I confess I should be delighted to meet you. I have enclosed tickets for you, and your Aunt and Uncle, to come to Great Falls where I shall meet you. I have to meet with my lawyers there soon anyway, so have arranged to do so on the morning your train should arrive. I do hope that you will come.*
>
> *I can understand your desire for family. Matthew and I lost our parents when we were young, but like you went to live with our cousins. My cousin Tom in fact lives here in Sun River, he runs the local Saloon. If he had not come here I doubt Matthew would have considered the place. It is small, but growing rapidly. Even since I arrived a further three homesteaders have arrived, and two more stores have opened in town. I like it a lot here, I hope you will too.*
>
> *I find I do not know what else to say to you, and pray that I will not be so tongue-tied when you and your family make your visit. It would be a terrible waste of money to come all that way only to find I am a stammering imbecile!*
>
> *Yours Most Hopefully*
>
> *Aaron Simmons*

Frederica smiled and clutched the letter to her breast. Her heart was pounding. He was delightful, funny and smart. She glanced at the tickets, the train left in just a few days. She couldn't ask her family to drop everything at such short notice, whoever would take care of the farm whilst they were gone? She would have to write and decline, maybe he would understand if she tried to reschedule the tickets?

"Frederica, was the letter from your beau?" Aunt Marian asked as she entered the pretty parlor and sat opposite her. She nodded. "You look sad, I do hope he hasn't snubbed you."

"No, quite the opposite," she admitted. She didn't want to show her the tickets, but Aunt Marian's sharp eyes rarely missed anything.

"He has sent you a train ticket? That is quite serious. I presume he intends to ensure all proprieties are taken care of?"

"He sent tickets for us all," Frederica said sadly.

"How wonderful. It would be rather nice to see Montana. I hear it is quite beautiful." Silently Frederica handed her the tickets, expecting her to gasp at the inappropriateness of the date of travel. She was simply too deflated to care what her prim Aunt might think of his being so presumptive. "Ahh," she said once she had read them carefully. "That may pose a slight problem. Give me a moment my dear." Frederica looked up. It seemed that there was something for her to be stunned by every single day with her Aunt these days. It sounded like her Aunt truly was on her side, and she had headed straight for the barn outside where she knew Uncle Frederick would be with the cows in calf.

Curious to see what was happening, under her nose, she got up and followed her. "Freddy, can we find someone to take care of the place while we do this? I should so like to make it up to dear Frederica. I have been such a shrew to her at times." Uncle Frederick laughed and put his arm around his wife. Frederica stared, open-mouthed as he bent down and kissed her gently on the cheek.

"My dear, I am sure I can arrange something. There is a gentleman who once enquired about buying the land. He wasn't sure if he wished to have a dairy herd here, but I am sure he could be prevailed upon to care for them until we can make arrangements. I shall contact him and find out if he is still interested."

"We do not need to sell up in just a few days, but we do need someone to mind it while we are gone," Aunt Marian said, her face a little stricken at the speed in which her husband was making such plans.

"Marian, do you truly wish to remain here? The site of all your biggest pain? You said just the other night that if you could leave tomorrow you would be glad to do so. This is such an opportunity for us all. I am tired, have worked hard my entire life. We have good savings, and the price we could achieve for this place could mean we could live a very comfortable life in somewhere like Montana, if we decided we liked it there. You hate this farm, it is the very reminder of everything that has been bad in both our lives. Why should we not move quickly to put it all behind us?"

"We have been making such progress together," she admitted.

"But it seems so much to give up. Both of us have never lived anywhere else, and know nothing else but this life."

"I am sure we can learn, adapt. And it would mean that if darling Frederica marries her young man we could be near her, to see her little ones born."

"I should certainly like that," Marian admitted. "I do hope she will allow us to be involved in her life though. What if she wishes to escape from us completely?"

Frederica was so touched at the lengths both of them were prepared to go to for her, and she emerged from her hiding place in the shadows. "I will admit, when I first advertised that was my purpose," she said frankly. "But things have changed here since then, we have all changed. I would be honored to have you nearby, a part of my life and my children's, if I am so blessed. But I am not sure I can ask you to give up everything you have worked so hard for all your lives on a whim."

"Neither of us has been happy here Frederica," Marian said.

"There was too much history, too much pain here," Frederick added. "I think we shall both be glad to see the back of the old place."

"Then I should send word and pray that it reaches Mr Simmons before we do!" Frederica said happily. She rushed forward to hug her Uncle, and then her Aunt. "It will be a new start for us whatever occurs."

The next few days passed in a flurry of packing. She and Aunt Marian flew through the house, marking the things they wished to keep; those that they needed to take with them to Montana now, and those which were to be kept in storage if Uncle Frederick could organize a buyer for the farm. They also threw away more things than they could have imagined, the old farm house was filled with the possessions of two families after all. Most of the items they discovered in the attics bore no familiarity to either of them. Uncle Frederick spent his days in Boston, at his club and with his lawyer as they tried to find someone who might wish to purchase it.

"My darlings, the gentleman I spoke of is still interested. We finally found him!" he cried as he burst through the door, the night before they were to leave. He had clearly indulged in a few too many glasses of port, but neither she nor Aunt Marian scolded him. It was wonderful to see him so happy. "We signed the papers today, and the funds are with my lawyers as we speak. They will hold them until we decide what to do next."

"Splendid news, but now we must all get a good night's sleep," said Aunt Marian. "We have a long journey ahead of us." They all nodded, and meekly followed her up the stairs. Frederica was about to head into her bed chamber when Aunt Marian stopped her. "Are you sure this is what you want?" she asked kindly.

"I am," she admitted. "Are you?"

"Oh, I am sure I shall learn to live with your Uncle as well in Montana as I would here. I think he is right, that we need somewhere completely new – with no bad memories – so we can have the very best chance."

"I pray it will be so for us all. Goodnight Aunt," she said and reached out to hug her Aunt close. Marian resisted for a moment, but Frederica was over the moon when she felt the older woman relax into the embrace, and hugged her back.

"Good night, my dear. I am sure I shan't sleep a wink. I am not sure if I am excited or petrified," her aunt confessed.

Frederica closed her door, and leant her head against it. She felt much the same way. She longed for a new start, prayed that Aaron was as good a man as she hoped. But she had fears too. He was a clever man, used to a way of living that was fast and exciting. She was not sure that he truly would be able to adapt to the quiet life he professed to desire. But, she admonished herself, she had requested a man with a sense of adventure. Yet, she had not expected that a man whose entire life had been made up of the kind of experiences that his had, would ever respond to her advertisement. There was much to be fearful of, not least that he might decide upon meeting her that she was too dowdy and not for him at all.

Slowly she prepared herself for bed. This would be the last time she ever slept in this bed, in this house. She gazed around the large and airy room, at the trunks tucked neatly against one wall and wondered what the next chapter of her life might hold. She sat on the bed, her knees tucked up under her chin, unable to sleep as thoughts ran amok in her mind. She found herself wondering what Aaron might look like. They had not shared any details about themselves in that way in their letters. What if he thought her ugly? She knew she was not fashionably pretty, but her long blonde hair had been commented on by many. But she knew that many men wanted their wives to be demure, dainty and a little needy. She was none of those things. Her years on the farm had given her strong muscles, and a lithe and capable body. She was not one to wait for anyone to rescue her and she was all too opinionated. Well, she had not said she was anything else in her correspondence, and so she could only pray that he wanted such a bride. It would be altogether too humiliating to be rebuffed now.

Chapter Five

Aaron paced anxiously up and down the station platform in Great Falls. His meeting with the lawyers that morning had been most productive, and he was now the proud owner-to-be of one hundred and sixty acres of land adjacent to his brother's farm. It would not belong to him for five years, but when it did he would have some of the best grazing land in the region for his dairy herds to roam on. The train whistled, a long and loud hoot as it approached the station. He couldn't help but think of all the journeys he had taken himself upon these great iron beasts. He felt a pang at the thought that he would never again be setting off to explore pastures new, to investigate and report on dangerous and ruthless people. A part of him was glad of it, but there was still an urge to do so even now.

As the train came to a halt, the brakes screeching and the pistons groaning, he took a deep breath. He almost choked as his lungs filled with smoke and steam. Spluttering, he narrowed his eyes and tried to make out the people as they disembarked in the haze. He didn't know what he was looking for. He knew only that she was coming. He had never been so nervous, not even when he had faced down Johnny Malone, the hitman sent to kill him. But that was his past, and today was all about his future.

A tap on his shoulder made him jump. "Mr Simmons?" an

elderly gentleman beamed at him. He nodded. "Sorry, didn't mean to scare you. I am Frederick Milton. This is my wife Marian," he indicated to a slender woman with a thin-lipped smile and wary eyes, "and my dearest niece, Frederica." Aaron turned a little to see the young woman he was indicating. She was struggling with a large trunk, and trying to bat away a porter who was offering to assist her. He smiled. He had expected she was determined, and independent from her having placed the advertisement, but he had not expected her to be so very beautiful. He moved towards her, as if drawn there by magnetism.

"Miss Milton, it might be best to let the porter help you," he said with a grin. "It is their job after all."

"What business is it of yours," she retorted. Clearly she hadn't seen her Uncle and Aunt approach him. "I am more than capable."

"I am sure you are, "Aaron chuckled. "But, if you were hoping that dealing with your luggage might put off the fateful moment when you meet Mr Simmons, then I am afraid you are too late." She looked up at him aghast.

"You are Mr Simmons?"

"I am, and do call me Aaron Miss Milton."

"Oh my, whatever must you think of me. I just got so nervous. I wanted to just get right back on the train," she admitted, glancing down demurely. She had the longest lashes, and they swept along the line of her cheekbone delightfully. He tilted her head back to his, and she opened her mouth as if to speak, but then stopped.

"I am nervous too, if that helps at all," he admitted. "But I still think we should let the porter do his job. They really are ever so good at it!" She smiled at him, and he felt a pang of desire for her light up inside of him. She had the most adorable dimples. He longed to be able to kiss them both, then her luscious pink lips until they both forgot all about being scared of one another. "Your Aunt and Uncle are waiting for us," he said stepping back from her. Standing so close he could smell the lemon in her hair, and a scent of lavender soap. It was quite delightful and very distracting. "We should make our way home."

The drive back to Sun River was slightly less uncomfortable. Uncle Frederic turned out to be a wonderful raconteur, and he regaled the stories of the people they had met on their journey across the country wonderfully. "Sir, might I spend some time with you once you are settled, to write some of these down?" Aaron asked. He was sure that many editors would love to have such a series of tales to print in their newspapers, about the types of people who made the move from East to West. Interest in such pioneers never seemed to wane.

"Of course my boy. Would be delighted," Frederick boomed. He was a charming and colorful character and Aaron was sure that he and the older gentleman would become fast friends.

Frederica and Aunt Marian sat quietly in the back, clearly they were used to being Frederick's audience but Aaron found himself wishing that Frederica would speak just a little more. She had a lovely lilting voice when she did, slightly deeper than most. He found himself bizarrely wondering if she sang at all, was sure if she did that her low alto would be most pleasing. Though he needed to keep his eye upon the often rutted roads, he took his chances to sneak a glimpse of her whenever he could. She seemed utterly overwhelmed by the beauty of the landscape; her face was a picture of pleasure. It made him happy to see it.

He pulled up, finally, outside his cousin's house. Tom and Catherine had agreed to put the trio up until something more suitable could be found. "Welcome," Catherine called as she stood up, their newborn baby in her arms. "I am so glad you have made it safe and sound."

"The journey was most interesting, if Mr Milton's stories are to be believed," Aaron said with a grin.

"You must not mind Uncle Frederick," Frederica said as she jumped from the wagon, not waiting for anyone to assist her. "He likes the sound of his own voice, and he does tell a good tale." He chuckled at the deftness of her movement, and the lightness of her landing.

"You must meet Claude," he said, not thinking that she wouldn't know who he was talking of. "I think the pair of you may get on well." She looked at him quizzically and Catherine laughed.

"It is a compliment, I think," she said. "Aaron was admiring your elegant jump. Claude is a Circus donkey. He does all sorts of tricks, and his owner, Emily does all kinds of acrobatics on his back."

"Oh, I see," she said, but Aaron could see she was still puzzled.

"You shall meet him later," Aaron said softly. "You are all

invited to supper at ours tonight."

"That will be lovely," Aunt Marian said firmly. "But, I do not know about my dear niece, or my husband, but I am getting on in years and am quite fatigued from our journey. Might I please be permitted a few hours rest before we do anything else?" Her family smiled at her.

"Of course," Frederick said putting an arm around her and lifting her from the wagon as if she were as light as a feather. "I should think we could all benefit from a good wash and a lie down."

"Follow me," Catherine said, a gentle smile playing over her lips.

"Well, that was the most romantic gesture I have ever seen between them," Frederica said. Her happiness was tangible.

"You said in your letters that they hadn't always gotten on so well?"

"No, in fact I thought they hated one another until recently. To be fair I believed Aunt Marian hated everyone, but it turns out they were both just unhappy. They are trying very hard to build a new life together. I have high hopes."

"I think you may be right to," he assured her. "Do you not wish to rest?"

"I have been sat on my derriere for weeks. I have done nothing but rest. Could we maybe go for a walk? I have been beginning to wonder if my legs even work!"

"I should be delighted. There is a charming stream behind the house, it leads up towards the river and there is a lovely little falls. I have been known to bathe there occasionally, as there is a delightful pool."

"That sounds perfect, and a swim sounds quite the thing on such a hot day." He gulped, just the thought of Frederica in the water, her hair slicked off her face, rivulets dripping down over her skin was enough to have him almost lose control. But he was determined not to scare her, wanted her to know that he was a gentleman and would never rush her into anything she did not desire.

"If you think you truly might like to swim, I can get Catherine to give us some bath sheets so we may dry ourselves? We could at the very least paddle, I think that could be seen as harmless enough," he teased.

"I am a grown woman Aaron. I have come here with the

intention of marrying you, I am not concerned for my reputation," she said bluntly as she set off in the direction he had pointed. He stood, marveling at how forthright she was, then rushed after her. Yes, he had been more than right to respond to that advertisement, and he found himself in a position he hadn't expected: he longed for her to be his bride, the sooner the better. He had liked her on paper, found her physically alluring, but this ferociously feisty young woman was more than he could ever have hoped for.

The scenery they walked through was stunning, but Aaron could barely tear his eyes from Frederica as they made their way up to the falls. She had a tiny waist, one he was sure he would be able to span with his hands if he were ever close enough to try, and gently curving hips that swayed as she walked. But she was also clever, and fascinating. She didn't just talk of clothes and hair and the other meaningless things so many women did. She was opinionated, like Catherine and Emily and she did not hold back on letting anyone know how she felt.

"Aaron," she asked him as they reached the pool. "Do you think we might suit? I know you have barely known me for five minutes, but I find myself oddly impatient." He stopped, and looked around, he could barely bring himself to look her in the eye. This was a question he should be asking her. "I am sorry, I do not mean to emasculate you," she added.

"Damn, woman!" he said. "How do you do that?"

"Do what?"

"Read my mind so easily. I was just thinking that I should have been the one to ask such a question!"

"I am terribly sorry, I am forthright – but even more so when I am nervous. You do not need to answer now, can wait until you know me better. I should not have asked."

"No, I don't mind," he admitted, surprised to find that he really didn't. She was refreshing. "But, we have shared only a few letters and a few words in person. There is more to a marriage than that."

"Whatever do you mean? Surely, the fact we get on is more than is evident in many marriages."

"I know you have seen unions that have stemmed from less than romantic beginnings, but I do not wish to be wed to someone I can merely tolerate," he said as he moved closer to her. She looked up at him, and he felt his heart beat faster. "Especially as I have a sneaking suspicion that I already feel a little more than that for you." He bent his head to hers, was delighted when she moved her lips to meet his. The kiss was soft, gentle but he could feel the heat inside him growing. He pulled her closer to him and ran his tongue across her lower lip. She breathed out in a heavy sigh, and parted her lips so he could plunder her mouth with his tongue.

"I have a sneaking suspicion I may feel a little more for you too," she whispered against his lips. Her arms wrapped around him, pulling him closer to her. He could feel every inch of her pressed against him, and it felt wonderful.

"Then I had best go and take a quick and cold dip before I take you back down to Catherine, so I can arrange a wedding with the minister as soon as possible," he said reluctantly pulling away from her.

"There is nobody here," she said wickedly. "Nobody who would see us."

"You are a temptress and a tease. Get away from me, I will not," he said trying to keep his tone light. "I will wed you first you little minx." She smiled at him, and he knew that he had just agreed to a life that would be more than exciting, every day would be a new adventure.

Chapter Six

Frederica wrapped her arms around herself and smiled. Every time she thought of Aaron, she pictured him dripping wet, emerging from that pool. His smile had been rueful as the water poured off his strong body. She had been half in love with him following his first letter to her, but the sight of him at the train station had left her utterly infatuated. He was beautiful, with his dark brown hair and long limbs. She hadn't followed her Uncle and Aunt to greet him as she had been sure that she would make an utter fool of herself, and so she had. Thankfully though, he seemed to be just as enamored with her as she was with him.

She shivered as she remembered his kiss. That delicious melding of lips, the warmth of his body against hers and the taste of his tongue still haunted her every waking and sleeping moment. But, from this morning that torment would be no more. By midday they would be man and wife, and she would be able to kiss him and touch him whenever she wished. She could not wait. She had never expected to fall so irrevocably in love with anyone, much less a man she knew so little of and yet she had. They had the rest of their lives to learn everything there was about one another.

"Are you ready?" Aunt Marian asked as she came into the chamber that Catherine had so kindly given over to her. "I have your dress."

"I am," she admitted as she took in the concoction of ivory silk and lace that her Aunt had labored over in the last week. "This is so beautiful," she said as she inspected the exquisite stitching and the tiny seed pearls on the bodice. "Thank you."

"It was my pleasure. Just be happier than your Uncle and I were, and your parents were my darling."

"I shall do my best, but it looks to me as though you and Uncle Frederick are more than making up for lost time," she teased. Aunt Marian blushed.

"We have purchased some land in Sun River; we will be building a house there as soon as Ardloe can do so. You will always be welcome."

"I know. Now, shall we get me into this dress and to the church?" Frederica held the gown up against herself and looked into the mirror. She had never looked happier. Her cheeks were flushed, and her eyes were bright. She felt beautiful for the first time in her life.

She walked down the stairs. Uncle Frederick had tears in his eyes. "Your Papa would have been so proud of you this day."

"I know, but are you? Am I making a wise choice? Everything is all so sudden," she said admitting her fears.

"He is a good man. He loves you. You will make it work — because that is who you are my darling."

"Then you had best take us to the church." She tucked her arm into his, and waited for Aunt Marian to join them.

Outside Tom waited on the dashboard of a smart open topped carriage bedecked in ribbons. "Well, my cousin is a lucky man," he said as they got inside.

The sunshine warmed Frederica's skin, though her hands stayed icily cold. She was sure it must be her nerves, but as they pulled up outside the church she suddenly felt calm. She knew she was doing the right thing. Inside, there was a man who made her heart sing, sent shivers of anticipation through her when she merely thought of him, and bolts of lightning when he took her in his arms and kissed her. There was simply no mistake to be made here, and when she glanced around at the faces of the family she would gain as Uncle Frederick escorted her down the aisle she knew that she had finally found happiness.

Aaron looked dashingly handsome in his suit, and wore a smile that warmed even her icy hands. When he took her hands in his she felt as if she was coming home, and she pronounced her vows proudly. He kissed her, as if nobody was looking, and she blushed when she remembered that they were still inside the church. It felt somehow blasphemous to be so focused on only him. They turned to face their new friends and family, and suddenly Aaron's smile faded. Frederica had never seen him angry, yet she was sure that was the emotion rushing through him as he took in a solitary figure at the back of the church. "Who is that?" she asked, feeling afraid.

"Someone I thought never to see," he admitted. "Stay with your Uncle and Aunt. Matthew and Tom will take care of you all. Go, now. Out through the vestry. Do not turn and look back, just go quickly. I have to know you are safe," he hissed at her.

He began to walk down the aisle towards the man, and Frederica went to follow him. But her way was blocked by Matthew. "Come, he will join us later," he said firmly.

"But whatever is happening?" she cried as he almost lifted her off her feet and dragged her away. "Why are you not staying to help him?"

"Because he always said that if the time came it was most important to him that you were safe."

"So, he told you something like this might happen, but not me? I am his wife!" she cried as Matthew finally set her down on her feet outside. Tom and Catherine followed with their baby, with Christopher and Emily not far behind. Uncle Frederick looked pale, and Aunt Marian furious as they joined them.

"I am to take you home," Matthew said to them all. "We need to stay together. There may be others watching. Do you have your rifle Tom?" he asked. Tom nodded.

"I have a pistol," Uncle Frederick said. "As does Marian. She is quite the shot."

"Why am I only learning this now?" Frederica said; everything she thought she knew was wrong, different. She didn't know what to think as she saw her Aunt pull a pistol from her reticule.

She didn't have time to think about any of it though, as they bundled into the carriage and raced out of town. But once they were at the farm, she began to wonder how even her Aunt and Uncle had been prepared for such an eventuality. How had they all kept this from her? Why had they kept it from her? She didn't understand what was happening, and she was more than scared for her husband. Frederica sat, and sobbed. She was wed to a man she barely knew, and she may be widowed just as suddenly as she had fallen in love with him. Was bad luck to follow her everywhere she went? It was not fair. How could this happen on her wedding day, of all days? She knew she was being selfish, should be standing up and fighting with everyone, but she felt so weak, so incapable of dealing with it all. What if he didn't survive? What if she never saw him alive again?

******

Aaron walked right up to Quent Treyhorne and stared at him. He stared back. He had clearly been on the run for a long time, he stank of sweat – both his own and his horse's. His stubble had grown out enough to almost be a full beard. Aaron wondered when he had last slept in a bed. "So, finally," he said. Treyhorne grimaced.

"Finally. Nice place this. Shame to see it ripped apart, just because of the likes of you," Quent said dryly.

"You won't be harming anyone here. You came for me, so let's deal with this once and for all."

"Nah, I don't think so." Treyhorne spat on the floor, right by Aaron's foot. "I think I might stick around and get me a nice little wife. I believe there'll be a young widow in need of comforting right soon."

"Over my dead body."

"That was the plan!" He chuckled at his own wit. Aaron gritted his teeth. He had to keep this man away from his family, had to keep him talking so that Sheriff Partlin could get here and see he faced the justice he deserved.

"Well, you might just find I am not the easy target you wished for all these years."

"I know that, you've always been too wily for your own damn good," he said bitterly.

"You alone?" Aaron asked, trying to sound nonchalant.

"Think I am that much of a fool as to open up to you about where my men are?"

"Yes, actually," Aaron said and laughed. "I think if you had any of the gang left at all that at least one of them would be standing right by your side now, and that I would have heard gunfire as my friends and family left the church." A curious look crossed over the outlaw's face. Aaron wasn't sure if he was angry, or just confused. He had never been too bright, but what he lacked in wit, he had more than made up for in brutality. Aaron was surprised he didn't already have a bullet lodged in his chest. Treyhorne was big on shooting first and worrying about it later. "Why are you here Quent?"

"To get my revenge. You ruined my life."

"No, you ruined your own life, I just wrote about it."

"Smart, ya always thought you was so smart," he sneered.

"Smarter than you," Sheriff Partlin said as he entered the church, and his deputy slapped the manacles on to Treyhorne. "He at least thought to warn the authorities you might not be far behind him so's we could all be ready with a nice cozy cell for you."

"You coward," Treyhorne yelled as he was led away. "I'll get you, see if I don't!"

"You had your chance, could have done it at any time since you walked into my wedding – but you didn't. You won't get another one," Aaron called back.

He leant against the pew, as he gasped for breath. He had done everything he could to appear calm, but he knew how close he had come this time. If it weren't for Treyhorne's arrogance he could have been dead. But he knew that facing Treyhorne would be nothing compared to what he would face at home. Frederica was not the kind of woman to take kindly to having been kept in the dark. But it was better to face it now, and so he did his best to stop shaking, and went outside to find himself a horse.

Epilogue

He raced up to the farm, part of him glad that he would be able to tell them all that everything would be alright, but the other part petrified that he had finally found the woman he wanted with every part of his being, only to lose her because of his own stupidity. But, he had his reasons for keeping it from her, he just prayed she would understand. As he reached the screen door he could hear his brother taking charge. Matthew had always been good in a crisis.

"Are you alright?" Matthew asked Frederica tenderly. She almost choked on the sardonic laugh his question created in her. Aaron felt his heart almost break at the fear and worry he must have caused her. He saw the pain on her face through the door and wanted to run to her, but he wasn't ready. He didn't know what he could possibly say to make it up to her.

"Will someone, anyone tell me what is going on?" she said, feeling almost hysterical. Matthew sat down beside her and put his arm around her. He was warm and solid and Aaron knew firsthand that his big brother could be very calming. He could see her face soften a little as she grew less anxious.

"You know Aaron was a journalist?"

"Yes of course, I read some of his pieces. They were ever so good, but he truly did write about some terribly dangerous people."

"Yes he did, and most of them ended up either hung or behind bars where they belonged. But, there was one man, the head of a rather brutal organization, who evaded capture. He has followed Aaron for years. He is not a pleasant man, but we hoped he wouldn't trace Aaron here to Sun River. But, I suppose with both Tom and I here, it was bound to be a place he would locate eventually. We have been prepared for him to come for Aaron, we had to be."

"But he let us come here, let my Aunt and Uncle come here knowing he might have to face this monster?"

Aaron clenched his fists, gritted his teeth and walked through the door. It was not fair that others make excuses for him to his wife. He should be the one to soothe her fears, all their fears. As he walked into the room everybody gasped. "Oh my goodness, you're alive!" Tom cried clapping him on the back. Matthew simply stood up and walked towards him. He wrapped him in his arms silently.

"I think we should leave Aaron and Frederica alone," Catherine said sagely. Everybody nodded and made their way out of the room. Young Christpher stopped and flung his arms around his Uncle's leg.

"I am glad you are safe," he said, a tear rolling down his chubby cheek. Aaron wiped it away.

"I am glad you are safe too," Frederica said once they were alone in a quiet, icy voice. He fell to his knees before her, took her hands in his and pleaded with his eyes. He could only hope that what he said now would be enough to exonerate him in her eyes.

"I know I should have told you," he started slowly. "And I hate myself for that. I truly believed I was finally safe, that he wouldn't find me here and I didn't want to worry you. I was here for so long, and there was no sign of him. He has always caught my tail so quickly in the past."

"But, why didn't you tell me. You told everyone else, and it would seem even my Aunt and Uncle, why not tell me?"

"I do not know. I love you so very much, and I did not want to give you any reason to leave me. I guess I was scared that you wouldn't want to run the risk of being with a man who jumps every time a door bangs unexpectedly in the wind, or spooks every time I hear there is a stranger in town."

"I would have understood. If I had known I could have been prepared."

"If you had known you would have tried to fight him yourself!" Aaron observed wryly. She smiled weakly at his joke.

"You are probably right."

"Can you honestly say you would have left the church as you did today if you had known?"

"No, I cannot. But it still does not mean I should have been the last to know. I have spent every minute since thinking I must be a widow. I will not live that way Aaron," she said firmly.

"I do not expect you to. There is nobody else out there, as far as I know, who is after my blood. But, please I beg you to forgive me. I love you, cannot live without you."

"I am sure I can learn to," she said her smile finally broadening, her dimples revealing themselves in all their glory. He kissed them and then claimed her lips. "After all, if an unhappy marriage like my Uncle and Aunt's can be turned around in such a short time I am sure there is hope for us."

The End

Thank you for reading and supporting my book and I hope you enjoyed it.

Please will you do me a favor and leave a review so I'll know whether you liked it or not, it would be very much appreciated, thank you.

Other books by Karla

Faith Creek Brides #1 (handwritten)

SUN RIVER BRIDES SERIES

A bride for Carlton #1
A bride for Mackenzie #2
A bride for Ethan #3
A bride for Thomas #4 ✓ (handwritten check)
A bride for Mathew #5
A bride for Daniel #6
A bride for William #7 ✓ (handwritten check)
A bride for Aaron #8 ✓ (handwritten check)
A bride for Gideon #9

SILVER RIVER BRIDES SERIES

Mail Order Bride Amelia #1
Mail Order Bride Camille #2

About Karla Gracey

Karla Gracey was born with a very creative imagination and a love for creating stories that will inspire and warm people's hearts. She has always been attracted to historical romance including mail order bride stories with strong willed women. Her characters are easy to relate to and you feel as if you know them personally. Whether you enjoy action, adventure, romance, mystery, suspense or drama- she makes sure there is something for everyone in her historical romance stories!

CPSIA information can be obtained
at www.ICGtesting.com
Printed in the USA
LVHW092040280321
682767LV00024B/577